I0626566

STOLEN HOURS

MICHELLE M. PILLOW

MichellePillow.com

Stolen Hours © Copyright 2010-2018, Michelle M. Pillow

Third Electronic Printing April 2018, The Raven Books LLC

Second Electronic Printing September 2013

Part Two, First Electronic Printing August 2011

Part One, First Electronic Printing January 2010

ISBN-13: 978-1-62501-199-2

Contents

About Stolen Hours

PARANORMAL GHOST ROMANCE

Homeless, jobless and manless, Helen Gettsman doesn't have a choice but to move into her inheritance in Nowhere, Oklahoma and make herself at home in the dusty, old mansion that is a drafty shadow of what it had once been. From the very beginning it becomes clear a house is not the only thing Aunt Susan left her. It would seem she now has the title of Caretaker and a new man in her life that died 100 years ago. Henry Gregory might welcome her presence, but not all the undead residents are happy about her staying.

This is a short story.

Note from the Author

This story was originally published in two parts. The first part was featured in *Paranormal Underground Magazine*; and the second in the *Mammoth Book of Hot Romance*, a multi-author print collection published by Running Press (US) and Robinson Publishing (UK) in 2011.

Michelle's Bestselling Series

SHAPE-SHIFTER ROMANCES

Dragon Lords Series

Barbarian Prince
Perfect Prince
Dark Prince
Warrior Prince
His Highness The Duke
The Stubborn Lord
The Reluctant Lord
The Impatient Lord
The Dragon's Queen

Lords of the Var Series

The Savage King
The Playful Prince
The Bound Prince
The Rogue Prince
The Pirate Prince

––––––––

Captured by a Dragon-Shifter Series

Determined Prince
Rebellious Prince
Stranded with the Cajun
Hunted by the Dragon
Mischievous Prince
Headstrong Prince

––––––––

Space Lords Series

His Frost Maiden
His Fire Maiden

His Metal Maiden

His Earth Maiden

His Woodland Maiden

———

To learn more about the books and to stay up to date on the latest news visit MichellePillow.com

To JRA: Happy Birthday

Part One

Chapter One

Nowhere, Oklahoma

Aunt Susan had always been a little eccentric — from her fast cars and reckless driving, her numerous seedy businesses and even more numerous marriages, to the sprawling three-story mansion on the hill. It had been commissioned and designed before the turn of the 20th Century by a friend of an ancestor.

The designer had died the day the last stone was set — or so the story went. Helen's great-grandfather moved in the next day. There was speculation as to whether or not foul play was involved due to money owed the architect, but nothing was ever proven.

Now, homeless, jobless, manless, Helen

Gettsman didn't have a choice but to open the dusty, old mansion, a drafty shadow of what it had once been, and make herself at home. She hadn't been back since her Aunt died, leaving it to her in a will. The money attached to the house drew enough interest to cover taxes each year and little else. Helen had hoped the place would sell. It didn't. Buyers wouldn't even go inside.

She had no desire to live in Nowhere, the aptly named ghost town of a place, with a population of 83 — if the decades-old sign was to be believed. But what choice did she have? The economy was in the toilet, her apartment building was sold by a bankrupt landlord, and her boyfriend of three weeks dumped her. No surprise on the last one. He wasn't really a keeper —more like a placeholder.

Outside, snow covered the ground, resting heavy on treetops and shrubs like the props of a postcard photo shoot. Aside from the rare trail of animal tracks, the snow lay untouched. Inside, the house looked as it must have been upon building, though age and wear had taken its toll. Only a few modern advances had been added — electricity, updated plumbing, and radiant heat.

Pictures of her ancestors and their friends

lined the walls and fireplace mantel. She'd studied their faces, not recognizing any of them. There was one man who'd captured her attention —in his old fashioned clothing and happy smile. The house was being constructed behind him, and on the back of the frame she'd read the words, "Henry Gregory, Architect, 1909."

Now, as she sat huddled on the musty couch, staring at the radiant heat vents encircling the bottom edge of the walls, she wondered if she'd made the right decision. The pink frills of her aunt's robe smelled of bourbon and cigarettes, but it was warm and counteracted the cool draft leaking in from the old windows. There were no neighbors, no television, no cable to hook a television to should she unpack hers.

But if there was no television, where exactly were the soft voices coming from?

Helen had been hearing them all day — giggles and whispers, floorboard creaks and groans. At first, as she unpacked, she was able to ignore them as the unfamiliar sounds of a new home. Though now, as she noticed the candlelight flicker on the wall, she wasn't so sure. She'd heard urban legends of people living in the walls of old homes.

Wait. Candle? She didn't light any candles. Twisting on the couch, she looked over her shoulder. The light flicker was gone.

"Probably just a trick of the evening light on the snow reflecting in the window," she said, the sound of her voice odd in the quiet place. She began to hum softly, keeping the silence away.

"There. See."

Helen paused, listening hard. "Hello?"

No one answered. Did she really expect them to?

"What the hell did my aunt do out here all day? It's no wonder she stocked enough liquor to fuel a frat party." Helen stood, hugging the robe to her chest as she made her way through the house. This was one heck of a way to spend New Year's Eve.

Shuffling her feet, she went toward what she thought of as the wall of liquor. Nearly every known brand had been crammed into the pantry shelves. "No champagne? Fine, how about, um, this?" She pulled out a half empty bottle of bourbon. "We'll toast to Susan. Seems fitting considering this is my new life."

The liquid sloshed as she stepped toward the cupboard to find a glass. The floor creaked behind her and she swore she heard a soft giggle. Helen turned, looking carefully into every shadowed corner within her eye line. Nothing. No one.

Giving a nervous laugh, she muttered, "Stupid drafty house."

She reached for a glass.

"Drafty? This design is..." This time the voice was louder and decidedly male.

Helen gasped, dropping the glass. It crashed on the floor, breaking into several pieces. "Who's there?"

Though she waited what had to be several minutes, nobody answered. Laughing nervously, she cleaned up the broken glass and threw it away. She kept a cautious eye on her surroundings, even peeking out the window to see if there were tracks in the snow. The sun had begun to set, casting shadows on the ground.

Carrying the bottle under her arm, she wandered into the dining room. The long table hardly seemed fitting for a household of one. Above her head was a chandelier with frozen glass droplets raining down. Just as she looked away, the light fixture moved, the glass droplets tingling lightly together. She chuckled, almost feeling relief. That had to be one mystery solved. The draft hit the fixture and caused a noise.

She set the glass down and poured a tiny bit. Sniffing the liquor, she wrinkled her nose. Heady and strong, it burned her nostrils. Knowing she might regret it, she tipped the glass back and drank. Fire burned down to her belly and she coughed, hacking at the unexpected pain.

"Just wait."

She gasped for breath, turning to grab the bottle to put it away. When she reached for the glass, she saw it had been filled to where she'd had it before. "What the...?" The burning had subsided some, but she still tasted the drink. She leaned over to look under the table. Nothing. Overhead the chandelier clanked.

Leaving the glass where it was, she backed out of the dining room. "It's official. I'm going crazy." She walked toward the living room intent on plugging in the old radio she'd seen earlier. Helen turned the knob, gliding the dial over the stations. All of them seemed to be playing old songs — waltzes and big band music.

Then, finally finding the faint strains of a country song, she turned up the volume.

Just as she was stepping away, big band

music blasted her from behind as one station seemed to take over another's airwaves. She jumped at the loud beat of horns and instantly turned the volume back down.

At first, she just listened, letting the songs flood together. Then detecting a vaguely familiar beat, she found herself swaying around the room. She began to kick, stepping back and forward with circling hands to reenact the days of the flapper. The frills on the robe bounced.

The radio signal fuzzed and a voice said, "What is that?" before the music once more took over. It fuzzed again and another voice answered, "I haven't seen anything like that before."

Helen paused. The conversational tone didn't seem like a radio show. Was she getting cell phone signals? Curious, she went to the radio and turned the dial.

The music faded but didn't disappear. The talking became louder.

"I do not think she is a good fit for us," a woman said.

"I think she's pretty," a male voice answered. He had a thick British accent and the deep timbre of it made her toes curl.

"Pretty?" A nauseatingly disgusting laugh

followed the woman's incredulous question. "Common, you mean..."

"Modern," the male corrected. Helen leaned closer, wondering who they were.

"Wait, is she listening? She knows!" the woman gasped. A cold, stiff breeze hit Helen's back, and she heard the unmistakable sound of footfall running out of the room. Helen jumped back and let loose a small scream. There was no denying the tingling of her flesh or the sound or running feet. She held her arms tight to her stomach, not daring to move as she glanced around the empty room. No one was there. She was alone in the house.

"They planned to greet you at midnight."

Helen made a small noise of fear. Was the British man talking to her? She didn't want to look.

"Susan has spoken very highly of you. She says you're the last of your family line. It's too bad really. You're family has always been kind to us."

"Susan?" Helen whispered. Then, closing her eyes tight, she said, "This is not happening. You're sleeping. You're drunk. You're —"

"Drunk after that small drink? Not quite, Miss Helen."

"You're sleeping," she told herself.

"This will go so much easier if you calm yourself. You will not be harmed. You're the new caretaker."

Footsteps sounded, boots on wood, and she swore they moved around the room with the voice. "I don't remember Susan being like this."

"Susan was crazy," Helen said before catching herself.

"Ah, so you are listening to me!"

"Go away."

"I can't." The man's tone was droll. "I live here."

"Isn't there a light? Shoo, get out of here, go toward the light." She relaxed some, though she still wasn't convinced she was lucid. "There's, ah, good, um, things in the light." The man laughed, the tone slightly mocking but mostly humored.

Helen finally managed to open her eyes and look toward the sound. Her pulse quickened. A transparent figure leaned against the doorframe, a crooked smile on his lips. His dark dinner jacket, white shirt, and dark tie looked turn of the 20th Century Edwardian style.

Laced-up leather boots and a felt Bowler hat with rounded crown completed the look. He reached for the hat, holding it before him by the crown, to reveal brown hair and even browner eyes. She stared through his chest, seeing the other side of the room.

He glanced behind him as if to see what she stared at and chuckled. "I assure you, I'm really here." This time when he spoke, his voice sounded fuller, solid. "In fact, I've been here for some time."

"You look like that picture of the architect," she said.

"I am that architect," he answered with a slight tilt of his head, "Henry Gregory."

"Henry Gregory is dead."

"Yes, I am. Exactly a hundred years ago come midnight." He brushed his hand absently over his suit. "I think the years have been kind if I do say so myself."

Was it her or was the house colder? Hearing a faint laughter in the other room, Helen frowned, looking past him. "What is that?"

"It's almost time." His body faded until it disappeared and she frowned.

"Time?" she repeated, taking a step toward

where she'd seen him. She rubbed the bridge of her nose and shivered. Had she gone completely mad?

"For the party," he said, this time from right behind her.

Helen gasped, jumping slightly.

"It's almost time for you to meet your wards." He motioned toward the doorway he so recently vacated.

"My wards?" Had someone told her that morning she'd be talking to a ghost, she would have laughed in their face. It wasn't that she didn't believe, just that she didn't believe them to be so...forthcoming.

The man leaned closer, and she felt a cool tingle on her face. He was handsome, and his eyes were kind. She shivered, automatically reaching to touch his face to see if she could feel him. Her fingers fell through his cheek, and he closed his eyes briefly. Her hand tingled and she withdrew it, hesitating midair.

Somewhere in the house a loud clock chimed the midnight hour. She stared at him, watching as his features filled in. His smile became full and his eyes solid. Her hand moved forward to his cheek once more. This time, she felt him, still cool but as solid as flesh.

Before she could ask about it, she heard a loud cheering, as if a crowd of voices suddenly erupted in the dining room.

His hand captured hers. "Come. Meet your family and their friends. They're all here, generations of them come to celebrate the new year."

Helen jerked her hand away as he tried to pull her with him to the door. "But, I'm not dressed. I'm..." She shrugged out of the pink frilly robe, hating the fact that she wore pajama pants and a T-shirt.

He just smiled, grabbing hold of her once more as he whisked her toward her strange new future.

Part Two

Chapter One

Thirteen Months Later...

"Get out, get out, get out!" Helen covered her
ears, trying to block out the rush of voices that
punctured her thoughts like tiny needles. The
chorus of words seemed to rain down on her, an
omniscient presence she couldn't quite block out
and the harder she tried to, the louder her houseguests became—all three dozen or so of them.
Well, 'guests' wasn't exactly accurate. In truth,
some had lived in the house before her and some
were those who'd died nearby. The house was
built near limestone and an underground stream.
Both elements attracted the spirits and gave them
energy. Now that the ghosts were enjoying their
afterlives, they still believed they had a right to

the place and she was their new caretaker. Apparently to some, caretaker equaled indentured servant.

Though she couldn't see them all, she knew they were there. They appeared as shadows and white mists, as tiny orbs of light, as full intelligent apparitions and as an endless looping of a single unaware activity. She heard them giggling and running, singing and dancing, usually just beyond the corner of her sight. They moved her belongings, creaked floorboards, jingled the crystal chandelier, made her paranoid to use the bathroom and essentially killed any chance she had at bringing a man home—not that there was a man to be found in the town of Nowhere, Oklahoma with its population of about eighty-three. Before she knew about the house's quirks she had tried to sell the place, but the realtor couldn't even get prospective buyers to tour the property. Whenever she tried to sell antiques to earn income, she met with protests. That is why it was so important she kept her online blogger job and she couldn't work with the constant demands on her time.

Not bothering to look up from her desk to the transparent people before her, Helen said,

"Fiona, I've already told you I can't do anything about the big band music. You have to fight it out with Bella, quietly and outside. Every time I throw the radio out, you all just bring it back. If you don't stop bringing this argument to me, I'll introduce you to heavy metal and turn it up so loud I won't be able to hear you ever again."

Helen knew the girls didn't know what heavy metal was but was beyond the point of caring. One of the girls whispered to the other, "She said she was going to drop metal on herself so she can be dead, too."

"Oh, no," the other answered. "Then who will be the caretaker?"

Helen kept her eyes on the desk, continuing on to the next of the houseguests' list of demands, "Jack, I won't cook liver-and-onions for you the next time you take corporeal form. You never eat them and they stink up the house. Plus, the last thing I want to be doing in the middle of the night while you all run around and party is cook. It's bad enough that you all only become corporeal in the middle of the night and without forewarning.

"Winston, I'm sure running a machine that removes the fuzz off of peaches was a fine career, but you're no longer in the northeast. This is Oklahoma. I need a job I can do in Oklahoma. So, for the last time, I am not rejecting your suggestion, it is merely impossible."

This time she did raise her eyes to a crotchety old ghost. He had his thumbs tucked into the sides of his overalls while he rocked on his bare feet. Every time he got worked up, scorch marks appeared on his wrinkled features. They were a reminder of the night his moonshine still exploded. "As for you, Jerry, please stop telling everyone there are demonic ghosts moving into the attic. We all know you died three sheets to the wind and when you get worked up you go into alcoholic delusions."

Jerry's face blistered down the side of his cheek and neck, the horrific sight disturbing but no longer scary. He stumbled to the side and then disappeared through a wall. Next to him, twins Bella and Fiona giggled. The two eternally ten-year-old girls were always arguing over who was technically older. Bella was born first, but also died of scarlet fever first. Fiona, having lived ten days longer than her sister, tried to claim elder status. They chimed in cherubic unison, "We love you, Miss Gettsman." At Helen's stern look, they ran through the door, the sound of their giggles and loud footsteps echoing behind them.

The snow had begun to melt and the constant beat of dripping water tapped outside the window as it fell from the roof. Beyond the window, old trees and thick shrubs dotted the rolling hills. They were shaded with the light of late evening. Normally, when the ground wasn't a vast puddle of mud, the surrounding landscape looked like something off of a postcard. Inside the isolated three-story mansion appeared close to what it must have looked like when it was built at the turn of the twentieth century, though the long years had taken their toll. Her late aunt had updated very few things, but luckily electricity and plumbing had been among them.

There wasn't much by the way of furniture. When she first came to the mansion, Helen had moved a lot of the old furniture to the barn to be refinished. A few of the spirits had some skill in that department. Though getting them to work was another thing altogether and the progress they were making was very slow. She supposed when one had an eternity ahead of them, they weren't in such a hurry. Her redecorating was another point of contention in the house.

Pictures of her ancestors and their friends lined the walls and fireplace mantel. She studied their faces, recognizing several of them as residents. Wryly, she muttered, "From living alone to over thirty vocal roommates. Thanks for the inheritance, Aunt Susan. You couldn't have just been the crazy recluse we all thought you to be and left me a normal house?"

Strangely, Aunt Susan was one ghost who hadn't appeared.

"What do you mean normal? There is absolutely nothing wrong with my house. The design is perfect."

Helen couldn't help the small smile that formed on her lips. She couldn't see him, but she knew that British accent well. One of the pictures caught and held her attention. It was of the house during its construction. In the foreground a man stood, smiling in a way that made her heart flutter just a little. The happy expression shone from his dark eyes, radiating in such a way that whoever looked found themselves smiling back. He'd been a friend of her great-grandfather.

Henry Gregory, Architect, 1909.

"Hello, Gregory," she said softly. An orange

light flickered, as if coming from a candle that wasn't there. The floorboards creaked and the faint sound of violins drifted in from far away only to fade. She pushed up from her desk, reaching to close her laptop's lid. "Where have you been? I missed you."

"Have I been gone?" The sound was fuller than before and more directional. She found Gregory standing in the doorway leading into the dining room. The turn of the twentieth century Edwardian style dinner jacket, stark white shirt and dark tie were the same as the day he'd died. Laced up leather boots and a felt Bowler hat with rounded crown completed the look.

Helen could see a chair through his transparent waist and caught herself staring at it. When her eyes darted up to his face, his crooked smile sent a shiver over her. Since the very first moment he appeared...well, no, to be fair, the first moment he appeared had been a little surreal. To be more accurate, since the first time she could look at him without freaking out about the fact ghosts existed, her house was haunted and she was what they called a caretaker, he'd made her pulse quicken. She was a fool and she knew it. Though he was an intelligent haunting, aware of her and their surroundings, he was a hundred years dead. She was thirty years alive. Nothing could come of them and she wasn't even sure how he felt about it, or if he could even feel as she did. Gregory was a gentleman from a lost era. His polite charm, the very thing that made her legs tremble and her desires rise, was merely a byproduct of his time.

Gregory pulled the hat from his head, holding it with strong, tapering fingers. Energy snapped from his movements, as if life was there beneath the surface waiting to burst forth. He smoothed his brown hair back from his face and stared at her with even browner eyes. When he was near the other voices seemed to fade. She suspected his spirit had been here the longest, as he died the day the last stone was set on the house. Helen's great-grandfather moved in the next day.

Gregory looked at his hand, lifting it as if to reassure himself he was still materialized. "I'm still here."

She'd been staring again. Clearing her throat, Helen said, "Sorry. I was wondering about something, ah..."

"Yes." His body blurred, drifting gracefully

only to pause once he stood before her. Her breath caught slightly and she wondered if he knew what his presence did to her. The very subtle hint of cologne wafted over her. He must have been wearing it the day he died, just like the fine suit.

"I know this might be a sensitive subject and..." Helen took a deep breath, trying to concentrate. She wondered if he knew how her body heated or that an ache low in her belly begged for release. "And if you don't want to answer, I'll understand."

"You want to know why I didn't kiss you last time I was corporeal." His hand cupped her cheek and for a moment, she stood stunned by the somewhat intimate touch. She had thought he might, as he'd stared at her with fading eyes, but she'd convinced herself she'd imagined the moment.

"Can you feel such things being that you are a...?" Her words were low and halting. But, now, as the tortured depths of his gaze, raw with emotion, bore into her and begged her to give him an answer to some unasked question, she knew what she'd seen was real.

"A ghost?" he finished when she couldn't.

"Yes. I can feel things as deeply as I did in life. Some of the others are locked in an emotion, as was I for a time. But, now, I can feel emotions. I can feel sensations against my body, though I can't feel as I do when I'm corporeal. I have come to believe that death is merely a transfer of energy. I am still me, but not as I was."

Helen longed for the solid feel of flesh, for the heat that radiated between two people. She longed for him to be of flesh and bone. However, those corporeal moments were fleeting, stolen hours in the night. Some people called it the witching hour, those brief minutes when the dead could play upon the earth once again—not every night, not every ghost, but some. Her nerves tingled in awareness, but she couldn't feel him, not like she could a live man, not now while daylight still found its way inside. She wanted to grab him, have him press her against a wall, have his lips against hers. Closing her eyes, she answered belatedly, "I wasn't going to ask about that. I was going to ask about something else."

"I wish to explain." His words had grown softer. "I need to explain. I haven't been able to rest since I saw that look in your eyes as I disappeared. I never meant to hurt you."

The sensation of him surrounded her, like hands hovering over her flesh refusing to touch. Frustration mingled with sharp awareness. If she concentrated, she could tell exactly where his essence brushed over her flesh. His hand touched her arm, slid up her shoulder and along her throat. She moved her head to the side, allowing him access. A thumb drew along her cheek, dipping beneath the surface.

"I didn't kiss you because it would be torture to stop and my time was at an end," Gregory whispered. She blinked, opening her eyes. His face was close, but he had no breath to hit upon her lips. "Since you arrived a little over a year ago to be our new caretaker, I have tried to..." He looked away, before briefly finishing, "I tried."

Helen wasn't sure how to answer. All she knew was that her heart pounded in her chest and she felt hot and cold at the same time. A shadow moved through the corner of her vision, but she ignored it.

"I don't know if you can even feel me now." He moved his fingers through her lips. "When I touch you, it's like an electric current that draws me in." He reached for her hand and she lifted it, holding it between them. Gregory pushed his hand through hers. Helen curled her fingers, desperate to hold him but unable to. Her senses were heightened, focused completely on him. "There yet just beyond my grasp, real but fleeting."

"I can feel you." She swallowed nervously. The chandelier crystals crashed together in the next room, reminding her of a wind chime. "You're tingling and cool."

Helen's entire body ached with the need to feel. To touch was such a simple thing, often taken for granted, and she couldn't even manage that. His nearness only made the rising desires worse, but she didn't ask him to leave. Where his fingers traced hers, a shiver traveled down her hand. It drew a wayward line through her arm, across her breasts to peak her nipples, only to center deep in her belly. Her legs trembled. Her breath deepened. Her heart raced.

Wanting. Needing.

Denial.

Helen almost cried out. Instead, she whispered, "When will you become corporeal?"

"Shh," he said. "We can't talk here. Not about this. The others are watching us. They're always around. They're trying to listen even now. We must find a place away from them."

Helen turned her head as another shadow passed by.

"Look at her," a disembodied woman's voice whispered. *"I told you she wasn't a good fit."*

"She is no caretaker," a male answered. Helen recognized Samuel, which meant the whispering woman was probably Rebecca. The spirit followed Rebecca around like a supernatural henchman. *"She doesn't understand the rules."*

"Gregory is one of us," Rebecca responded. *"It is time she learns that. This goes too far."* A nauseatingly disgusting laugh followed the comment.

"What are they talking about?" Helen asked. When she turned her attention back to Gregory, she realized he was gone.

Chapter Two

Helen retreated to the only place in the house the ghosts couldn't materialize—her second story bedroom. The Victorian four poster bed, antique furniture and lavishly woven rugs over the wood slat floors created an opulent feel. When she first spent the night in the bedroom, she'd had visions of being a fine lady. That was until she'd woken up to find two men playing cards at the foot of her bed. They'd looked at her like it was the most normal thing in the world. She'd screamed so loud and long the two of them hadn't reappeared for nearly six months. A salt barrier went down the next day.

A grandmotherly spirit had been kind enough to point out the instructions Aunt

Susan had left Helen on how to protect her bedroom and keep the houseguests out. Apparently, she wasn't the first caretaker to have privacy issues. Though sounds of footsteps and whispers sometimes drifted in, the salt she'd poured kept the others out. There were times when she considered salting the entire estate. Only, to do so would banish Gregory with the others.

Helen glanced into the hall, placing her hands on the doorframe as she leaned out. The lady in white walked past, not noticing anything around her before fading mid-stride. Telling time by the consistency of the lady's daily stroll, Helen knew it would be just after five o'clock. "Gregory? Are you here? Where did you go?"

She felt him before she saw him. It was a brush of cool air again her cheek. She pulled back into the room. He stood on the threshold, unable to enter. Without speaking, she knelt down on the floor and brushed her hand over the thin line of salt to sweep it away. Before she could stand, he passed over her, entering. Helen drew her finger, redrawing a crooked line with the salt.

"You're trapping me in your room?" Gregory asked, though he hardly appeared concerned.

The thud of running feet sounded overhead followed by a hard crash.

Helen pushed the door closed as she stood and listened for the latch to click. The room suddenly felt very small. "I can't believe we're alone." Heat warmed her cheeks. "It seems strange. I wasn't sure you'd come in here, but you said we needed a place the others couldn't see so we could talk."

He looked around the room. His features blurred slightly. "Why would you think that? You've never asked me to come in here."

"You being a gentleman and all." Helen motioned at his clothing, noting the way he carried himself. These traits were a constant reminder. "I feel myself compelled to act like a lady, only I'm not sure how a lady acts."

At that he chuckled. "I've been around for quite some time. Just because I only own one suit during my afterlife, doesn't mean I haven't changed. I don't expect women to be like the ladies of my time and I don't expect you to be anything but you."

"There is something I've been dying to know. Earlier, I was going to ask about your death. The family legend says you died of foul play because my great-grandfather owed you money. Is that true?"

"You think Frank killed me?" He chuckled. "No, it wasn't that, it was an accident. I was pushing the workers to finish on time and stopped to check on the progress before going to a dinner party with your great-grandfather. One second I was looking up at my creation, the next I was standing dazed in the middle of the parlor watching people walk right by who couldn't see me. They say the suddenness of my death is what kept me here, just like the others. Those who die naturally seem to take the option to move on to wherever it is spirits go."

"Honestly, it's kind of a relief. I couldn't stand the thought of a relative of mine having killed you over money." She gave a nervous laugh.

Within a breath, he was close. Tingling erupted on her flesh. She tried to steady her nerves, but her hands trembled. A thought whispered through the back of her mind, telling her this was insane. It didn't matter. Her entire life she'd felt like she was sleepwalking through the world. Now, in this secluded place in Oklahoma surrounded by ghosts, she felt more real than ever before. Gregory made her feel alive. She could no more banish him from her than she could stop breathing.

"I need to sit down," she whispered. "I have to hold on to something or I'll fall."

Helen walked weak-kneed to the bed. Gregory appeared next to her. His weight didn't shift the mattress, but the bed did shake a little. The harsh pant of her breath echoed around them. She reached for his face, her fingers tingling as they went through his neck. "I don't know if I can do this." He began to pull away. "I meant not being able to grab ahold of you. I can't remember wanting anything more. Tell me this isn't crazy, that I'm not locked away in some mental institution due to hallucinations."

Gregory shook his head. "As I've told you before, this is all very real. Though, I cannot attest to this place not being an asylum. You have met the residents."

Helen laughed.

"Lie back and close your eyes," Gregory urged. She slowly obeyed.

Sensations filled her, overwhelming her senses. He stretched out next to her, his body pushing into hers and causing it to tingle. A hand swept over her hip and down her outer thigh, the caress like a teasing feather over her skin. Her breath caught and she focused on his touch. There was no need to remove her clothes, she felt him as if she were naked. Parting her lips, she took a deep breath. With each weightless caress, her body heated more until she was squirming beneath him.

Moisture gathered between her thighs. Helen ground her heels into the bed, longing to have something firm pressing into her. She wanted to run her hands into his hair, to hear his breath echoing hers, to feel his lips and tongue and teeth against her mouth. The sensation of his hand slid along her inner thigh, bringing pleasurable torment with it. She tensed as he drew close to her sex, wondering what it would feel like to have him there.

Helen felt a tug at her shirt. At first it didn't register, as her mind stayed focused on her stomach and thighs. He tugged again. This time more insistently as he tried to pull the shirt over her head. She blinked, focusing on his face. The color of pale flesh had begun to fill in the transparency of his expression. He pulled at her shirt, trying to grasp the material with fingers that could not hold them. Helen made a move to help, tugging the shirt over her head and tossing it aside. As soon as she'd finished, Gregory touched her skin. The sensation felt warmer, thicker.

"What's happening?" Helen reached for his face and met with solidifying flesh. The color of tanned skin replaced the pale, as if painted across his features. It filled in his lips, darkened his eyes until his gaze penetrated her with the full force of his desire. His hand pressed into her stomach. She gasped. It answered the call of her desires and was the most wondrous thing she'd ever felt.

Without questioning further, she knocked the bowler hat from his head and reached for his tie, pulling his mouth to hers. She sighed against the firm press of his lips. This was the moment she'd waited so desperately for. Her passion grew with each brush of their bodies. She pulled off his tie and slid her hands into the front of his jacket, pushing it from his shoulders. It fell next to them on the bed. The subtle musk of cologne emanated from his neck as she kissed a trail from his mouth to his ear.

Her hands fumbled as she unbuttoned first his shirt and then his old fashioned under garments. Helen wasn't sure why she was so nervous. She'd known him for over a year, talked to him for endless hours. They'd discussed old books and customs. She'd told him of movies and the marvels of technology. They relayed stories of youth, of past loves, of all those little things friends talk about and can't really remember discussing later. She knew his face, his smile—though normally she knew them to be transparent. She knew the sound of his voice, how it sent chills over her each time she heard it.

And, now, as the material of his clothes parted, she knew the feel of his stomach against hers. Breath rushed against her cheek as he inhaled against her. Heat radiated from his chest. Fingers revealed muscles, finding dips and curves once hidden. Their legs tangled and hips pressed until the unmistakable feel of his desire molded against her.

"How long will this last?" Helen rubbed her hand down his cheek and neck to travel over his shoulder. He leaned back and drew his arms out of his sleeves. A long scar cut across the smooth, strong flesh of his chest. He was a man who had worked during his lifetime, not only designing homes but building them with his hands. She liked his hands—sure and steady with the calluses of hard work.

"I do not know," he answered. Lids fell heavy over his eyes as he looked at her. His gaze lingered on her light green bra. "I have not done this since before my death."

Helen unbuttoned her pants and pushed them from her hips. Gregory leaned back on the bed, jerking them off her legs. Her lacy green panties matched the bra. He bit his lip to see them. Reaching for her hip, he pulled at the lacy barrier covering her sex. The panties glided down her legs and he dropped them next to the bed.

Urgency filled them. She had never seen him corporeal during the daylight hours and wasn't sure how much time they had until he disappeared again. His eyes focused on the thin line of hair standing guard over the slick folds of her sex. Gregory undid his pants. The material slung low on his tight hips, revealing the full length of his arousal. He caressed her legs, pulling them open so he could settle between her thighs. Helen reached for him, tugging his arm to draw him forward. His hand ventured up her inner thigh, moving until fingers glided along her pussy.

Helen gasped, arching her hips into his hand. His finger tested her response, dipping beyond the barrier of her sex. He entered her slowly before moving to rub the tight bundle of nerves hidden within the moist folds. Her hips jerked in response, a wholly involuntary movement that sent pleasure washing over her body.

His hair was soft as she ran her fingers into it. Her gaze traveled over his chest, following the thin scar, watching its subtle movements. She pulled his mouth to hers, moaning as she kissed him. Their tongues met eagerly. Gregory braced his weight on one arm and the sheer force of his solid body to hers made her shiver in anticipation.

He dipped another finger inside her and Helen thrust herself against his hand, trying to end the ache he stirred within her. She wanted him like she'd never wanted another. Her kiss became rough as she pushed up from the bed. The large bulge of his arousal brushed against her thigh and she tensed. Almost mindless in her desperation, she flung his hand away from her sex and grabbed hold of his hips.

He held his body tense. The first intimate touch forced a small cry from Helen's lips. The hard length of his cock filled her, slow and deep. Pleasure erupted, but it was bittersweet as tension and neediness soon followed. Gregory bit his lip, his entire body strained. He stayed embedded inside her, as if afraid to move.

Helen dug her hands into his shoulders, drawing her ass down into the mattress before pushing up. Her legs worked against his hips. Taking his cue, Gregory moved. He pulled out only to thrust deep. Helen needed more. She bucked beneath him, her body urging him with every subtle and not-so-subtle movement to give her more. They rocked their hips, seeking a natural rhythm that would alleviate their yearning desires.

Helen groaned. Her body was so close. She needed release so badly. Flipping him onto his back, she took over, riding him as she sought fulfillment. The new position gave her control over their movements. Gregory's fingers dislodged her bra as he grabbed her breasts. Electric sensations filled the hard peaks of her nipples as he pinched them lightly between his fingers. She lifted up only to fall down upon his lap.

Gregory groaned, grabbing her hips to keep the now frantic pace of her thrusts from slowing.

His gorgeous body strained beneath hers as he rocked up into her. His feet dug into the bed, forcing his cock deep. She gasped, panted, moaned. Clawing at his chest, she circled her hips. The tension became almost unbearable. Release was close, so close, so...

Helen cried out as she reached her climax. Her body jerked violently and she felt as if she couldn't catch her breath. Gregory thrust a few more times before he too found his release. Inside her sex a tingling sensation erupted where his body intimately touched hers. Before she could pull off him, she fell onto the mattress. She gasped, looking at the empty bed beneath her. Gone, too, were his disheveled clothing. He'd disappeared.

Breathing hard, she rolled onto her back. Her limbs tangled in her discarded clothes and mussed up bedding. Her heart thudded hard in her chest and sanity took a long time coming back. Helen stared at the ceiling, barely seeing it. The best sex of her life had been with a ghost who came so hard he'd disappeared. She gave a slight laugh, unsure whether or not she should be worried.

Chapter Three

Helen glanced around the living room to make sure she was alone before she quickly finished her purchase. She'd done her research and according to the ghost hunting websites she'd found, a device called an EMF pump would work as an energy source for ghosts. The theory was that entities could use the electromagnetic field to manifest more easily. It might be a long shot, but if she put one in her bedroom, maybe Gregory could...

She didn't finish the thought. Hearing an unfamiliar scraping noise, she frowned and shut the lid to her laptop. Someone was dragging something heavy across the floor. Suddenly, she was hit with a cold blast of air and her breath turned into a white puff as she exhaled. It had been awhile since the spirits affected her in such a way. Shivering, she rubbed her arms.

"Who is that?" she called. The hairs on the back of her neck prickled. Remembering the conversation she'd heard earlier, she asked, "Samuel? Rebecca? Is that you?"

The lights flickered. The dragging noise stopped.

"This isn't funny!" Helen yelled, making her way into the dining room. "Stop! I mean it."

Everything stopped for a brief couple of seconds. But, just as she was starting to breathe a sigh of relief, the lights began to turn on and off. Cabinets and doors opened and closed, banging loudly. The chandelier's crystals crashed together as the fixture swung violently on its base. A chair lifted off the ground, spinning in slow circles. Helen watched it as she edged toward the nearby stairwell. Suddenly, it was launched at her. She screamed, ducking as she ran. The chair crashed into the wall, splintering into several pieces.

"Who is this?" she cried stumbling to crawl up the stairs. Beneath her the first story floorboards creaked. "What do you want?"

Though, Helen suspected she knew what this was about. Gregory. They'd taken their relationship to the next level, defying the laws of mortality and afterlife. Even as they'd made love she'd worried about what it would mean. She hadn't seen him since it happened. Had the other's done something to him because of her? A knot of fear and worry tightened in her stomach.

The midnight hour fast approached and the spirits would only become stronger. A bitter wind whipped through the house as the front door flew open. The only thing she could think to do was get to the protection of her bedroom. Outside the country would go on for miles and the spirits could follow her if she tried to make a run for it.

As she neared the second story hall, the noise suddenly stopped. The silence was even eerier than the noises. Each of her steps was punctuated by the harsh sound of her breath. She pressed her arm against the wall, stepping as lightly as she could. A light glow appeared, slowly growing to form the lady in white. The ghost stepped silently through the hall. The midnight hour was here. When she reached the end of the hall, she disappeared, only to reappear and begin the walk again. The loop of her walk would last for about an hour. Though she knew the lady wouldn't deviate from her stroll, Helen pulled away from her as she passed.

The bedroom door was close. Helen reached for the doorknob. She studied the lady's serene face as she passed. The woman's eyes shifted, finding Helen against the wall. That had never happened. Without warning, the woman's mouth opened in a blur of movement. A loud screech blasted from the ghost's mouth as shadowed hands emerged from her chest. Whoever looked at her was not the lady. The lady in white kept walking as another figure emerged from within her.

Helen reached for the doorknob, shaking it as she tried to get it open. At first, the door didn't move. When she let go, it swung open. Gregory stood on the other side. His features suddenly turned white. A loud thwack sounded, denting his skull and sending blood streaming down his face. She automatically reached for him, but she felt something holding her back. He stumbled, falling to his knees and tipping over onto the floor. Helen breathed hard as his lifeless eyes faded. The door slammed in her face.

Helen stumbled to try and open in again, but the shadow creature flew toward her, hitting her body hard enough to knock her over as it passed through her. Dizzy, she grabbed her head, trying not to throw up as a wave of nausea washed over her. The shadow came at her again and again, draining her energy each time it passed through her body.

"Stop," she croaked. Helen crawled toward the stairwell leading toward the third story. She reached the bottom stair and the entity stopped. Tears streamed down her face. She tried to lift her body, but it was too hard to move. The hallway floorboards creaked. Helen pulled her knees toward her chest. Above her, someone stepped down the stairs, coming toward her head. A frozen breeze brushed over her, stinging her eyes.

"I knew you didn't fit here." Rebecca leaned over her, a dark red slash across her throat. Helen felt more than saw the others gathering around them. Samuel's dirty, transparent boots appeared by her head. "Gregory belongs to us. You are not one of us."

"So, what? You're going to kill me and make me one of you?" Helen asked, finding her strength. She pushed up. A horrifically disfigured gathering stared back, crowding into the hall and stairwell. It was hard to see past burnt flesh and bleeding gunshot wounds to the people beneath. Each one's story could be seen in their gaunt expressions and markings of death.

"Kill you?" Rebecca frowned. "We want you to leave here. Go. We don't need you. Gregory belongs to me. He's..."

"You?" Helen finally understood. Rebecca's jealousy washed over her. She'd suspected it once or twice, but Gregory never paid the woman much mind.

"Us," Rebecca corrected. It came a little too late. Fiona and Bella giggled. Jerry grunted and stumbled from behind Rebecca's back, falling through a wall. A young boy threw and invisible ball and ran away, chased by his ghostly parents.

"You're losing them," Helen said. A few of the grotesque figures mended, replaced by the peaceful countenance of the ghosts who normally roamed her halls.

Rebecca looked at the others, her throat reddening as she shouted, "She's trying to take Gregory from us. She trapped him in her room. She's using him!"

Rebecca's anger washed over Helen and she grasped at her chest. "Don't listen to her. Look at her. She's jealous. Don't let her hatred fuel you." Then, turning her full attention toward Rebecca, she stood, getting into the woman's transparent face. "You want Gregory for yourself. You're mad that he chose to come to my room. You're mad that he chose me. You want me gone, but I'm not leaving. You'll have to kill me first. But then you know I'll only be with him. He chose me, Rebecca."

"I can make your life here hell," Rebecca hissed. "You think tonight was bad, just wait."

"It's not right, caretaker," a normally quiet farmer said from behind Rebecca. He'd been shot in the chest. "You ought to stick to the living."

"Rebecca?" Samuel questioned, the sound slow. "What does she mean you want Gregory?"

Helen almost felt sorry for the brute. She heard the heartache in his voice.

"Shut your trap," Rebecca ordered the man.

Helen still felt weak but tried not to let it show. She stepped forward, past Rebecca into the remaining crowd of onlookers. The air was chilled, but not as bad as before.

"Let me by," she demanded, keeping her

voice low and exact. "This is my home now. If you want to remain welcome here, you will act with civility and respect toward me and each other. Otherwise, pack your supernatural bags and get out." A few bowed their heads and disappeared. A young woman in a party dress and an old man in his long pajamas stepped out of Helen's way.

"Then you must respect us and leave Gregory alone," Rebecca said. Samuel stared at Rebecca, his face a strange blue as water dripped out of his lips. Helen turned, meeting the woman's eyes.

"I can't do that," Helen answered. "I love him."

The door to her bedroom opened. The sound caused her to glance over her shoulder. More ghosts disappeared, clearing a pathway to her room.

"No!" Rebecca screamed, but the sound wasn't sustained as she disappeared.

Helen walked toward the room and peered through the opened door. Gregory stood on the other side. The late hour had given him enough energy to take shape. He looked as he had when she first saw him, standing with a crooked smile on his lips, hat in hand. He took a step as if to come to her, but stopped, staring at the floor. She glanced down to the line of salt, realizing he was indeed trapped.

Helen didn't step past the threshold.

"I am sorry for this. I tried to warn you but I couldn't leave this room." He lifted his hand, but couldn't touch her. "I didn't mean to leave you earlier. I couldn't maintain form. If I hurt you, I'm sorry."

"You didn't hurt me," she said, nervous.

"If you command it, I will leave and not come back, not during your lifetime. I have no right to steal the years of your life with my death. You deserve more than I can give you." He stepped away from the door. "First you must release me from this room."

"Did you hear what I said in the hall?" she asked, stepping carefully over the salt. She shut the door behind her, trapping them both in.

"I tried to warn you—"

"I said I love you, Gregory. I know this isn't conventional, but I love you. I don't know where we go from here, or how we make it work, but I do know I want it to work." She closed the distance between them and reached for his jacket. His body solidified as she touched him. "I've tried to deny any pull I feel toward you because I didn't know if you could feel anything for me. But, after today, after what we shared, I never want to be without you again."

"I'm dead," he said hesitantly. "You're alive."

"No relationship is perfect." She gave him a small smile. "Besides, I won't always be alive. Eventually, I'll die and then you'll be stuck with me for an eternity."

"Eternity," he repeated, dropping the hat. It landed with a thud on the floor. He pulled at his tie, loosening it. "I like the sound of that."

Helen backed slowly to the bed, beckoning him with her eyes. "People are going to think I'm a crazy recluse just like my aunt."

"What do you think?"

"I think I've finally found a place to call home. Let the world think what they like about me." Helen pulled him into her embrace. "This is what I want. You are what I want."

"And I want," he glanced down, "you to be sure when you do die that you're wearing that green lacy thing you had on earlier."

Helen gasped, hitting his shoulder as she pretended to be shocked. Grabbing hold of him, she fell back onto the mattress taking him with her. His body settled against hers and she felt his interest poking against her hip. She nipped at his earlobe. "Oh, I think you might change your mind when you see the other options available. Underwear has changed a lot since your time."

Gregory captured her mouth with his, silencing her with his passionate kiss. Happiness bubbled inside of her. Everything she could ever want was right here within the stolen hours in his arms.

The End

For a complete, up-to-date booklist, visit
www.MichellePillow.com

New York Times & *USA TODAY* Bestselling Author

Michelle loves to travel and try new things, whether it's a paranormal investigation of an old Vaudeville Theatre or climbing Mayan temples in Belize. She's addicted to movies and used to drive her mother crazy while quoting random scenes with her brother. Though it has yet to happen, her dream is to be a zombie in a horror movie. For the most part she can be found writing in her office with a cup of coffee while wearing pajama pants.

She loves to hear from readers. They can contact her through her website.

www.MichellePillow.com

facebook.com/AuthorMichellePillow

twitter.com/michellepillow

instagram.com/michellempillow

bookbub.com/authors/michelle-m-pillow

goodreads.com/Michelle_Pillow

amazon.com/author/michellepillow

youtube.com/michellepillow

pinterest.com/michellepillow

Author Updates

To stay informed about when a new book is
released sign up for updates:

http://michellepillow.com/author-updates/

Also By Michelle

THE DRAGON'S QUEEN

Dragon Lords Series
Bestselling Shape-shifter Romance

The Dragon's Queen Excerpt

There were three things Medellyn knew for a fact. She was special. She could kick the ass of any boy. And she did not want to marry and have babies.

She was special.

Medellyn was one of the only dragon-shifting females in all the universe, and definitely in all of the Draig. Only once in a thousand births was a female dragon-shifter born. She was rare, or so everyone kept telling her. Her childhood was a strange contradiction. Her very proper mother tried to treat her as if she were some sacred crystal that might crack. Her warrior father tried to make her train like a boy while dressing like a girl.

She could kick the ass of any boy.

Medellyn hated when boys tried to act as if she were weak and to be protected. Her dragon was just as fierce as any of theirs, probably more so. To prove her point, she'd gladly pummel any who had challenged her to the ground...and some who hadn't.

She *absolutely, positively* did not want to marry and have babies.

Being the special, rare creature she was, in the twenty not-so-sweet girlhood years of her life she'd been claimed as the future bride to nearly three dozen boys—each one confident that when they came of the age to marry she would make their crystals glow and they hers.

Glowing crystals wasn't just a metaphor. On the day she was born, her father journeyed to Crystal Lake like all the new fathers did. He dove beneath the waves, swam down to the deepest part and pulled her stone from the lakebed. Like all Draig children, she wore the stone around her neck, and would continue to wear it until the day it glowed telling her which of the dragon-shifting men she was destined by the gods to marry. Okay, technically she might be destined to marry an offworlder like most Draig men, but no one on her planet seemed to think so.

Gods bones, she hoped she wasn't destined to end up with any of the idiots on her planet. They had yet to impress her.

When it was her turn to go to the Breeding Festival, the crystal would glow signifying her *curse* for all to see. Well, her "blessing" as her mother called it. Lady Grace did not appreciate her daughter calling marriage a curse. Grace did not appreciate a lot of things that Medellyn liked, such as swords and bows, ceffyl riding, camping alone in the forest, hunting, sparring, smashing arrogant looks off of dragon men's faces.

It was a fight with her mother that sent her running through the mountain forest. Medellyn hated the woman, hated what her mother wanted her daughter to be. Grace was only a human, brought to their planet as a bartered bride. She married Medellyn's father without question and spent most of her days completely in docile agreement with whatever her husband said. Medellyn couldn't imagine taking anyone else's opinions over her own.

Her father, Axell, was a highly praised warrior in the Draig army and carried the title of Top Breeder of the ceffyls. The man's whole life focused on four things: his wife, his only child, and mares and steeds. Her father was a very important man, but his work kept him away from home several nights a week as he slept outdoors with the herd. With a three-year gestation period and only about fifty percent live-birth rate, the animals were not a resource that could be easily renewed. His ceffyls supplied the soldiers with mounts and farmers used them for beasts of burden to help with the fields.

Like Axell, Medellyn was a proud dragon. Had she been born male, she would have been a warrior, too. Instead, she was *special*. How could her human mother begin to understand the wildness than ran in her dragon blood? If she had, Grace would never have asked Medellyn to tame her spirit.

Breathing hard, she came to an abrupt halt and screamed into the trees. Her body shook with rage and she tore at the pretty gown she wore. She hated her body, hated being special, hated being expected to act like a lady when she felt like a dragon. Her taloned finger snagged on the crystal around her neck and she cut the leather strap of the necklace. The crystal flew several feet away.

"I am not some man's chattel," she yelled, knowing she'd run far enough away that her mother could not hear her retorts. Since she was shifted her voice was hoarse and powerful, and she reveled in the fierceness of it. "I am not some breeding ceffyl to have children. It is not my place to give you fifty grandkids. I can't help you only had one child. If you would have made me a boy, I wouldn't be a disappointment to you!"

Tears stung her eyes as Medellyn walked aimlessly, searching the forest floor for the fallen necklace. Finding it, she grabbed the inert crystal into her fist. It was a reminder of all she was expected to be. She took a deep breath, looking at her fist and then to the stones littering the forest floor. A small smile formed on her mouth. Medellyn dropped the crystal on the hard ground and glared at it. Rage boiled inside her, the kind of rage surely only a dragon-shifter could feel.

"This is what I think of your fate," she growled as she fell to her knees.

Medellyn grabbed a heavy rock and smashed it down onto her necklace. The crystal cracked. The noise gave her some satisfaction so she hit it again. Grunting with each strike of the stone, she didn't stop until her future had been ground to dust.

"That is what I think of your destiny."

To find out more about Michelle's books visit www.MichellePillow.com